Festivals
+
Celebrations

for Daisy and Flora

Copyright © 2002 by Mark Birchall

The rights of Mark Birchall to be identified as the author and illustrator of this
work have been asserted by him in accordance with the Copyright, Designs and Patents Act, 1988.
First published in Great Britain in 2002 by Andersen Press Ltd., 20 Vauxhall Bridge Road,
London SW1V 2SA. Published in Australia by Random House Australia Pty.,
20 Alfred Street, Milsons Point, Sydney, NSW 2061. All rights reserved.
Colour separated in Italy by Fotoriproduzioni Grafiche, Verona.
Printed and bound in Italy by Grafiche AZ, Verona.

10   9   8   7   6   5   4   3   2   1

British Library Cataloguing in Publication Data available.

ISBN 1 84270 079 0

This book has been printed on acid-free paper

Rabbit's Party Surprise

Mark Birchall

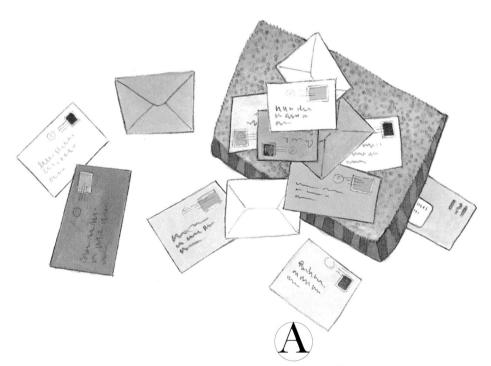

Ⓐ

Andersen Press
London

Rabbit was telling Mr Cuddles about her party.
"There'll be jelly with ice-cream and games with prizes," she said. "I hope you'll be coming."
Mr Cuddles didn't say a word but Rabbit knew that he'd be there.

"Come on, it's time to go shopping," said Mum.
"There's lots to get and I'll need your help."
So off they went.

They bought balloons and paper hats, crisps and
juice, a sticky carrot cake . . .

and much, much more.

"That must be everything," said Rabbit happily.

"Not quite," Mum told her. "There's still one more place to go."

And they went to book
The Amazing Ali Gator.
"Oooh, I love magic,"
said Rabbit. "I can't wait
for the show."

The Amazing Ali Gator
gave her a poster of himself
looking most impressive.

Rabbit carried it proudly home.

She helped Mum with the preparations.
At last everything was done.

The doorbell rang.

"Your friends are here," called Mum. "Now the party can begin."

"But I can't find Mr Cuddles,"
Rabbit cried.

"Where did you see him last?"
said Mum.

"I can't remember."

"Well, where have you looked?"

"Everywhere!"

"Never mind," said Mum.
"We don't have time to look now.
I'm sure we'll find him later."

But Rabbit didn't want
to party without Mr Cuddles.

She didn't want to play pass the parcel
or hide-and-seek.

But she couldn't help peeping when The Amazing
Ali Gator showed off his card tricks.

Or when he made Miss Flamingo disappear . . .

. . . then reappear in a different place altogether. Rabbit's friends cheered and clapped.

The Amazing Ali Gator bowed, then gave his hat a tap. And, hey presto . . .

"Mr Cuddles!" gasped Rabbit. "I *knew* you wouldn't miss my party!"

Everybody clapped again, but this time Rabbit clapped loudest of all . . .

"Hip, hip hooray for
The Amazing Mister Ali Gator!"